For Mom. For everything.

Once in a
Blue Moon

Danielle Daniel

Groundwood Books House of Anansi Press Toronto Berkeley

Once in a blue moon,
skipping in the sun,
I see not one but two rainbows
painted across the sky.

Once in a blue moon,
running through the woods,
I spot a hundred fireflies
blinking their bright lights.

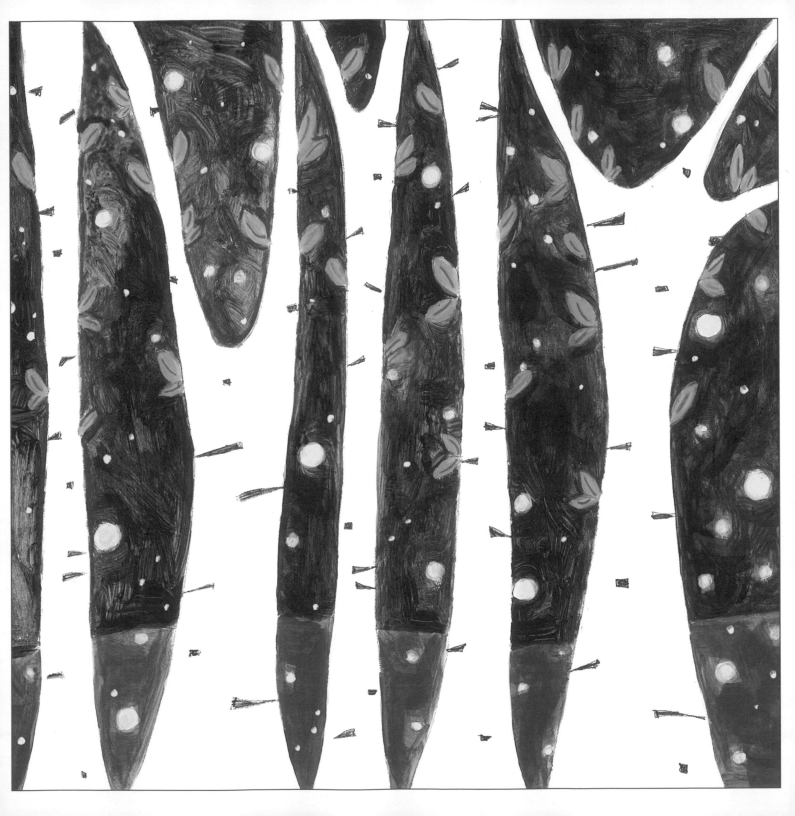

Once in a blue moon,
sitting very still,
I peek at a monarch butterfly
landing on my nose.

Once in a blue moon,
daydreaming by the pond,
I watch a painted turtle
basking on the rocks.

Once in a blue moon,
playing deep inside the forest,
I glimpse a large bald eagle
flying between the trees.

Once in a blue moon,
riding my red bike,
I spot a row of ducks
crossing the dirt road.

Once in a blue moon,
gazing up at night,
I see shimmering Northern Lights
dancing in the dark.

Once in a blue moon,
hiking through the park,
I find a four-leaf clover
hiding in the grass.

Once in a blue moon,
fishing in a boat,
I watch a massive whale
swimming alongside me.

Once in a blue moon,
picking flowers in the field,
I notice spotted ladybugs
resting on the leaves.

Once in a blue moon,
floating across the river,
I spy a large brown owl
hooting down at me.

Once in a blue moon,
exploring from my window,
I glimpse a shooting star
falling from the sky.

Once in a blue moon,
walking through the woods,
I spot a giant antlered moose
grazing by the lake.

Once in a blue moon,
hugging a large maple,
I feel its leafy branches
gently shading me.

Groundwood Books / House of Anansi Press
groundwoodbooks.com

We acknowledge for their financial support of our publishing program the Canada
Council for the Arts, the Ontario Arts Council and the Government of Canada.

Canada Council   Conseil des Arts
for the Arts   du Canada

ONTARIO ARTS COUNCIL
CONSEIL DES ARTS DE L'ONTARIO
an Ontario government agency
un organisme du gouvernement de l'Ontario

With the participation of the Government of Canada   Canadä
Avec la participation du gouvernement du Canada

Library and Archives Canada Cataloguing in Publication

Daniel, Danielle, author, illustrator
Once in a blue moon / Danielle Daniel.

Poems.
Issued in print and electronic formats.
ISBN 978-1-55498-975-1 (hardcover). — ISBN 978-1-55498-976-8 (PDF)

I. Title.

PS8607.A55645O53 2017   jC811'.6   C2017-900734-3
C2017-900735-1

The illustrations were done in acrylic gouache and pencil.
Design by Michael Solomon
Printed and bound in Malaysia